THE
MAGIC WINGS

THE MAGIC WINGS

A Tale From China · by Diane Wolkstein
illustrated by Robert Andrew Parker

E. P. DUTTON   NEW YORK

The story is based in part on the story line of "Growing Wings"
from *The Milky Way and Other Chinese Folk Tales* by Adet Lin,
published in 1960 by Harcourt Brace Jovanovich, Inc.

Unicorn is a registered trademark of E. P. Dutton.

Library of Congress number 83-1611
ISBN 0-14-054769-X

Published in the United States by E. P. Dutton,
a division of Penguin Books USA Inc.

Editor: Emilie McLeod   Designer: Riki Levinson

Printed in Hong Kong by South China Printing Co.
First Unicorn Edition 1986   W
10 9 8 7 6

for my mother,
Ruth Wolkstein,
who loves flowers
and has always delighted
in the impossible dream

There was once a little goose girl in China. She was a poor, ragged thing with no mother or father. She lived with her aunt, and every morning she led the geese out of the yard and up into the hills, and every evening she brought the geese back down to the yard.

One day in spring as she led the geese up the hill, she saw a tiny crocus pushing its way out of the earth. She bent over and watched. It seemed to grow before her eyes. The earth was damp. It had rained during the night. Then from the corner of her eyes she saw another crocus, and another. And another! She turned, and everywhere she looked, she saw new flowers pushing their way out of the earth.

"Hello!" they seemed to call to her. "Hello! Hello!"

The little girl started to run here and there, greeting each new bud and flower.

"Hello! Hello!" they called to her from all over the hillside.

"Hello!" Lilies, irises, clover, buttercups. But she could not run fast enough to greet each of them.

Just then one of her geese flapped its wings and lifted itself into the air. Ah, she thought, that is what I need to see all the flowers— *Wings.* If I had wings, I could fly over all the hillside and greet the spring!

Her thoughts returned to the earth, and she saw a little brook nearby. Quickly she ran to the brook, and cupping some water in her hands, she wet her shoulders. Then she stood very straight in a sunny place and slowly began to flap her arms in the air.

It happened that the grocer's daughter was on her way home from visiting a friend and passed the goose girl on the hill. When she saw the goose girl waving her arms up and down, she stopped.

"What are you doing?" she asked.

"I'm growing," the goose girl answered.

"Growing?"

"Yes. I'm growing wings so I can fly."

"You can't do that," the grocer's daughter said.

"Oh yes," the goose girl replied. "I've watered my shoulders, and soon my wings will sprout and I will fly over the world to greet the spring."

"I don't believe it," the grocer's daughter said. But when she got home, she thought, If a goose girl can fly, certainly a grocer's daughter can fly.

She went into the store and poured some milk into a bucket. She went outside and wet her shoulders with milk, stood in the sun, and slowly flapped her arms up and down in the air.

A judge's daughter was about to enter the grocer's shop when she saw the grocer's daughter waving her arms up and down in the air.

"What are you doing?" she asked.

"I'm growing."

"Growing?"

"Yes. I'm growing wings so I can fly."

"You can't do that," said the judge's daughter.

"Oh yes. The goose girl covered her shoulders with water, but I've covered mine with milk so my wings will sprout and I will fly over the world."

"I don't believe it," the judge's daughter said, and she went into the store. But as she walked home, she thought, If a grocer's daughter can fly, if a goose girl can fly, certainly a judge's daughter can fly!

At home she went down into the cellar, and looking for the oldest wine—wine is said to produce great miracles!—she poured a small amount into a glass and went outside. Then she wet her shoulders with the wine, stood in the sun, and slowly flapped her arms up and down in the air.

It was tiring, but she continued. And the grocer's daughter in town continued, and so did the goose girl on the hill.

It was a lovely day, and the princess decided to take a stroll through the upper parts of town. When she passed the judge's daughter standing on her terrace waving her arms in the air, she stopped.

"What are you doing?" the princess inquired.

"I'm growing," the judge's daughter answered.

"Growing?"

"Yes, I'm growing wings so I can fly."

"You can't fly."

"Yes, Your Majesty. The goose girl has wet her shoulders with water, the grocer's daughter with milk. But I have wet my shoulders with wine so my wings will sprout and soon I shall fly over the world."

"It is not to be believed," the princess replied. But immediately she thought to herself, If a judge's daughter can fly, if a grocer's daughter can fly, if a mere goose girl can fly, then certainly a princess can fly!

The princess returned to the palace. She went into her bedroom and poured her most precious perfume—does not perfume bring the gods to earth?—onto her shoulders. Then she stood on her balcony overlooking the town, and gracefully waved her arms up and down in the air. Waiting...

The queen stepped out onto her balcony and saw the princess flapping her arms in the air.

"Purple cushions!" the queen exclaimed. "Whatever are you doing?"

"Oh Mama, I am growing."

"*Growing?* My dear, you are completely grown."

"Yes, Mama, but I am growing wings."

"Wings? *To fly?*"

"Yes! Yes! The goose girl wet her shoulders with water, the grocer's daughter with milk, the judge's daughter with wine. But I have wet my shoulders with the finest perfume, so *I* shall be the one to fly!"

"Purple—" And the queen was about to say "dragons!" when it occurred to her that she, the queen, had never flown, and what if the princess, or worse yet, the judge's daughter, should fly before the queen?

The queen turned on her heels and strode through the palace to the royal treasury, where the sacred oil for crowning kings, queens, and emperors was kept. With brief ceremony and dignity, she anointed her shoulders with oil. Then she went out onto her balcony and began to flap her arms up and down in the air. Waiting...

When the girls and women of the town saw and heard about what the princess and queen were doing, they stopped what they were doing and wet their shoulders. Soon all the girls and women were standing in a sunny place, flapping their arms in the air. Waiting...

"Sister!"

"Mother!"

"Wife!"

"*Grandma!*"

The boys and men beseeched the girls and women.

"Speak to us!"

"Explain to us!"

"Tell us. What are you doing?"

But the girls and women were concentrating all their efforts on flapping their arms so they might fly.

In desperation the men and boys appealed to the Spirit in Heaven Who Grows Wings. The Spirit in Heaven Who Grows Wings heard their cry and had sympathy for their plight. It was impossible for life to continue happily, with the girls and women waiting eternally to fly.

The Spirit Who Grows Wings considered the matter and determined that one should be permitted to fly. But which one?

The Spirit descended to earth.

The Spirit flew from one girl to another, from one woman to another. The scent of the princess greatly attracted the Spirit, yet it could not be denied that certain grandmothers *were* trying very hard. The Spirit surveyed each girl and woman— the goose girl, the grocer's daughter, the judge's daughter, the princess (oh! the smell of the princess!), the queen....And, at last, the Spirit came up behind—

The little goose girl!

The goose girl felt a trembling behind her and a trembling all about her. A wind came. And suddenly she was sailing in the air, higher and higher and higher. She saw crocuses and lilies, roses and lady slippers, violets and daisies, star grass and buttercups—

The waiting was over. The goose girl who had wanted to greet the spring had been chosen. And all the people ran into the meadow to watch her fly.

"It's spring!" the birds sang.

"It's spring!" the people shouted.

"Hello!" the flowers called to the goose girl.

"Hello! Hello!" she called back. "It's spring!"

STORYTELLER'S NOTES

This story is wonderful fun when members of the audience join in acting it out. The five principal roles are the goose girl, the grocer's daughter, the judge's daughter, the princess, and the queen. The entire audience can also become the participating girls and women. *One precaution:* If you, the storyteller, intend to take the role of the Spirit Who Grows Wings, choose a lightweight girl or boy to be the goose girl.

The milk in the story is soybean milk. The wine is rice wine.